NORMAN

WRITTEN AND ILLUSTRATED BY
MICHELLE OLSON

Amazing stunts performed by Norman

PHOTOGRAPHY BY
BRIAN KESTER

Bellie Button
Books

For Thomas, Kaylee, and McKenna. Thank you for supporting my crazy ideas.

Bellie Button Books, LLC
belliebuttonbooks@gmail.com

Printed in the United States of America

First Printing, 2018

ISBN 978-1-7323707-0-8

Visit the author's website at www.michelle-olson.com

A big thanks to my editor Marlo Garnsworthy at www.WordyBirdStudio.com

Like all buttons, Norman was a sensible, well-rounded individual. He kept his coat closed, which meant his person was warm and comfortable. Norman felt needed, and that made him very happy.

But recently, Norman had been feeling a little down.

Norman felt completely lost.

Norman wandered aimlessly. The thought of his person feeling cold depressed him. He missed his coat and being needed. Norman was convinced a new job would help him feel needed again.

"What job does the world need most?" he thought.

A superhero, of course! Catching bad guys and foiling evil plots sounded perfect. Norman could transform into NORMAN the SUPER BUTTMAN! Ummm... or maybe just BUTTONMAN.

"This is a great idea!" Norman thought as he headed to his parents' house to get started.

Norman spent hours making his costume. But when he looked in the mirror, he was discouraged. He wasn't quite the superhero he had hoped to become. Sure, his new green underwear looked great, but his muscles just weren't big enough.

"I guess a button superhero does seem a *little* silly," he thought.

Norman hoped some fresh air would spark new job ideas. The mountains were inspiring, and Norman was sorry he had forgotten his camera. Then it dawned on him: he could be a photographer!

MARCH 2017

NATIONAL PHOTOGRAPHIC

PHOTO OF THE YEAR
GOES TO NORMAN
THE BUTTON 103

SEE THE WORLD
FROM A BUTTONS
PERSPECTIVE 23

TAKING PICTURES
WITHOUT FINGERS:
A BUTTONS GUIDE 78

People would love to see his unique view of the world, and that would certainly make him feel needed.

It turns out being that small really limits your viewpoint.

The magazine publishers laughed at Norman's photos. Apparently, people *don't* want to see things from a button's perspective.

Norman was determined to think of a great new job, even if he had to stay up all night.

In the glow of his backyard campfire Norman had his best idea yet. What about firefighting? That job was definitely needed. If cats got stuck in trees, he could only imagine how many cat-erpillars needed rescuing.

Norman soon learned two very important things: buttons are flammable, and he probably should have gone to

As Norman soaked in a cold bath to soothe his burns, he realized the bathtub was the answer. He could be a plumber!

Plumbers made bathtubs and toilets work, and everyone needed those.

It turned out that becoming a plumber was just a pipe dream. Norman began to wonder if there was any job he could do.

As Norman sat in the park, feeling depressed, he spotted a dog. Maybe being a dog-sitter would help him feel needed. He could take puppies on walks and read them bedtime stories.

Feeling rather happy about his decision, Norman hopped off his daisy and thought, "They're just dogs... How hard could it be?"

Apparently, it was very hard, especially for someone only two inches tall.

Norman had been laughed at, melted, nearly drowned, and dragged through the mud.

"I'm just not good at anything," he thought. "Maybe I should just give up."

As he waited to be recycled, Norman wondered what he would be turned into. The thought of no longer being a button brought tears to his eyes. What if they melted him into something gross like a toilet brush?

"I really need to stop being so emotional," Norman thought. "After all, I'm a button, and we're known for keeping things together."

That's right! Norman was a button, so why was he trying to be something else? No wonder he was failing at those other jobs. He needed a job only a button could do!

Norman felt new hope. He didn't know exactly how or where he would find his next job, but he felt he was getting closer. If he had a nose, certainly his next job would be right under it.

And of course, there it was, as obvious as the empty spot on that teddy bear's face.

Once again, he felt the happiness
of feeling needed. He finally found
his new job...

...and this time, he made sure he was double-knotted.

CPSIA information can be obtained
at www.ICGtesting.com
Printed in the USA
LVHW071010130119
603679LV00009B/9/P